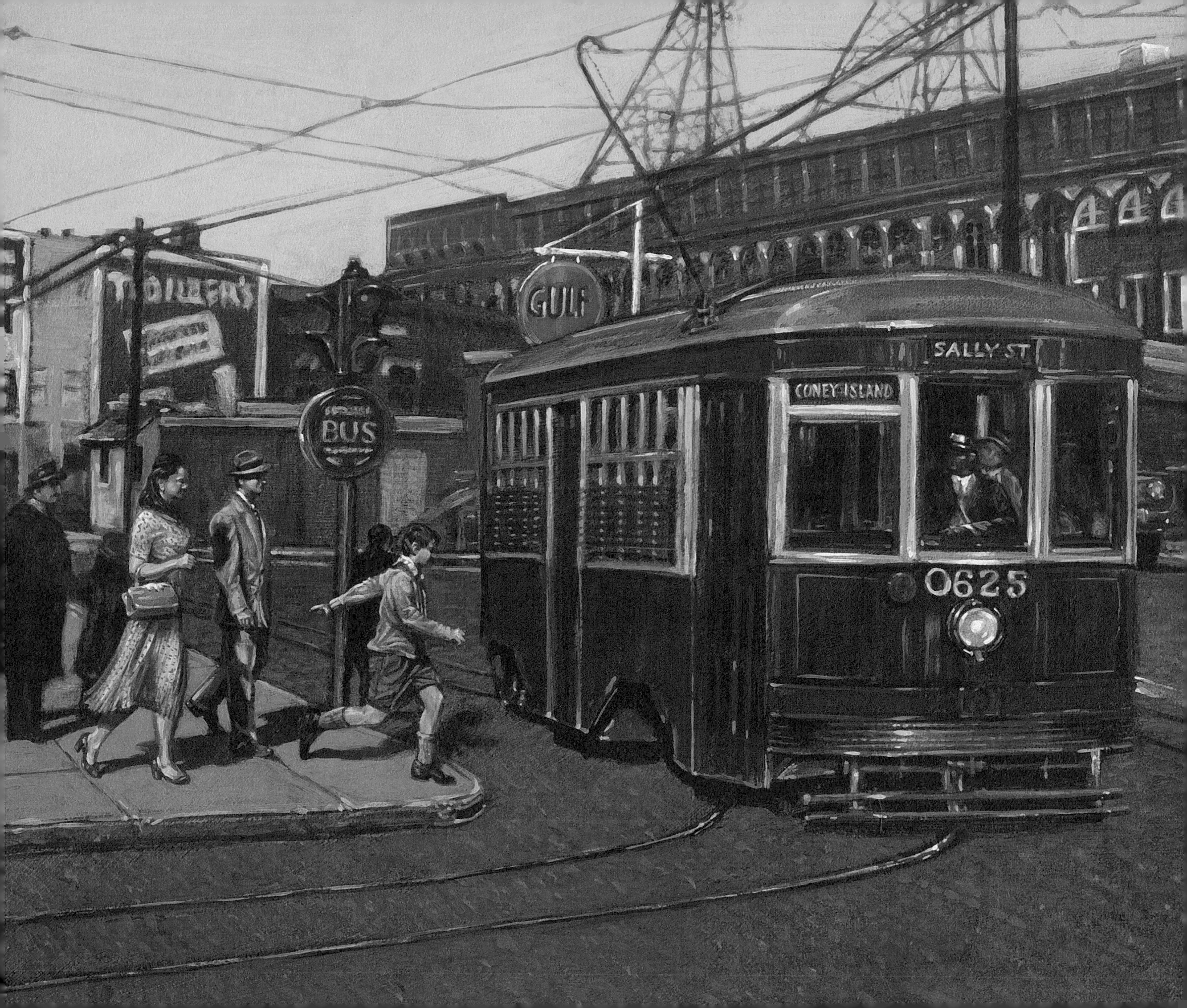
GULF
BUS
SALLY ST
CONEY ISLAND
0625

THE SOUND OF ALL THINGS

This book is dedicated to my grandsons,
Max Uhlberg and Miles Uhlberg.
One day, all grown up, you will take this book down and remember how much your Banka loved you, and how he told you stories about the time he was a boy in Brooklyn.

And, as always, to Karen,
who loved Louis and Sarah, and spoke with them
in their beautiful silent language.

—M. U.

This work is dedicated to my wife Drury and her endless patience; our newborn Tess and her joyous spirit; eldest daughter Sally and her wondrous light; and Sally's namesake, my mother, an outstanding botanical artist and lover of children and family.

—T. P.

Published by
PEACHTREE PUBLISHERS
1700 Chattahoochee Avenue
Atlanta, Georgia 30318-2112
www.peachtree-online.com

Design and composition by Loraine M. Joyner

The illustrations were rendered in gouache and acrylic on gessoed illustration board. Title and bylines are typeset in Kalenderblatt Grotesk by Dieter Steffmann for Typographer Mediengestaltung; text is typeset in Constantia by John Hudson for Microsoft Corporation.

Printed in November 2015 by Tien Wah Press in Malaysia

10 9 8 7 6 5 4 3 2 1
First Edition

ISBN 978-1-56145-833-2

Cataloging-in-Publication Data is available from the Library of Congress.

The Sound of All Things

Written by Myron Uhlberg
Illustrated by Ted Papoulas

PEACHTREE
ATLANTA

LIKE A CATERPILLAR, the roller coaster inched toward the top of the hill.

I looked at my father. Because he was deaf, he spoke with his hands, shaping words into pictures painted on the air.

"Tell me what the wheels sound like when we go down the hill," he signed.

I didn't have time to answer. Just then we fell down the shaking mountain.

I held my breath and clung hard to the safety bar, imagining that I was riding an angry dragon. Up and down we bumped and looped.

CYCLO
Island
ONE

Finally, the dragon slowed to a stop. "What did you hear?" my father signed.

"It was loud," I signed back.

"Many things are loud. Please tell me better."

I pointed at the clouds gathering overhead. "Heavy. Like thunder."

"Yes," he said. "I can feel that kind of noise."

My father and I stepped out of the car. My legs were as limp as two wet noodles.

Mother was waiting for us.

"It was wonderful," my father signed to her. "I could hear the wheels turning on the tracks through my hands and feet."

"The merry-go-round is more my speed," she signed in reply. My mother was deaf, too. Her signs were softer than my father's.

Ever since my father had lost his hearing as a young child, he had tried to use his other senses to understand sound. For as long as I could remember, he had been asking me to tell him what things sounded like. Sometimes I wanted to say no. It was hard to think of different ways to describe what I was hearing.

As the three of us walked toward the boardwalk, a strong breeze shook the leaves on the trees.

"I feel the wind," my father signed, "the way I feel your voice when you talk into the palm of my hand."

CANDY

The wind scattered the clouds, and the summer day grew even hotter. It seemed that all of Brooklyn had come to Coney Island to cool off.

We sat on a bench to watch the waves roll in.

"Look at how the sunlight is caught in the waves," my mother signed.

"Yes," my father answered. "I wonder how they sound."

"Why do you always want to know what things sound like?" my mother asked. "You and I will never hear them."

"But I will," he signed strongly. "In my mind."

My mother's hands sat silent in her lap.

"What do you hear?" my father asked me. "What does the ocean sound like?"

"It is loud," I answered again.

"Don't be lazy," he signed.

I squirmed in my seat. I didn't have enough words to tell my father what he wanted to know.

The wind had picked up again. A big wave came crashing onto the beach.

"What about now?" he asked. "When the ocean is angry?"

"It sounds...hard. Like a hammer." I banged my fist on the palm of my other hand.

He nodded in approval. "Good," he signed.

TICKETS
HOT DOGS
CANDYLAND
RAVEN HALL
COFFEE
POP CORN
CANDY
POP CORN

All around us, people swarmed over the boardwalk. They were talking and laughing and eating hot dogs and pink cotton candy.

A boy teased a girl by putting taffy in her hair. “Look what he did, Ma!” she screamed. “I’ll never get it out!”

“It was an accident,” the boy said.

I wished for a minute that I was like other kids. They didn’t have to explain things all the time to their fathers.

Storm clouds rolled back in, mountains of them, hiding the sun.

My father jumped to his feet. “Let’s go to our favorite Chinese place for dinner,” he signed.

The waiter greeted us and led us to a table. My father pulled out a notebook and wrote a few words on it. He showed it to the waiter, who then scribbled on his own pad in Chinese. My father pointed at the waiter's bold characters, and then at his own neat letters. Going through their usual routine, they each pretended to be confused.

My mother tried to keep a straight face. We both knew that my father and the waiter were old friends who understood each other perfectly. They enjoyed this ordering ceremony as much as the serving and eating part.

After we finished our dinner, I asked if we could go to the library. The Coney Island branch was right above the restaurant, and I knew it stayed open late some evenings.

As we walked through the door, I breathed in the smell of books and Chinese food.

I looked at the hundreds of books crowded on the shelves. They held as many words as there were grains of sand on Coney Island. This was surely the best place to find new words for explaining sounds to my father.

"What are you looking for, young man?" the librarian asked me.

"My father is deaf," I said. "I want to be able to tell him what waves sound like. Is there a book that can help me?"

SALLY

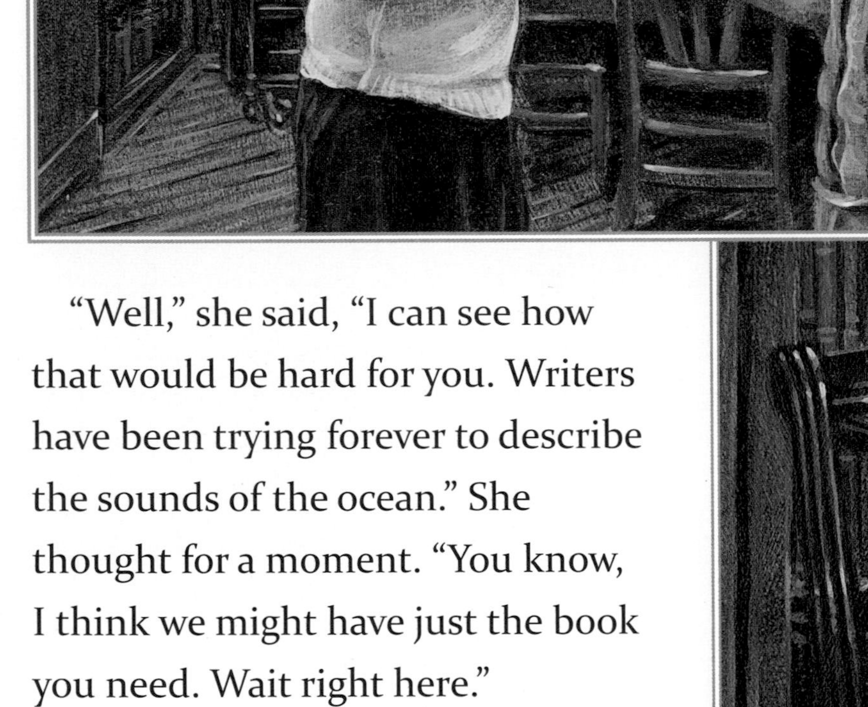

"Well," she said, "I can see how that would be hard for you. Writers have been trying forever to describe the sounds of the ocean." She thought for a moment. "You know, I think we might have just the book you need. Wait right here."

After a few minutes, the librarian returned. "This is one of my favorite poetry books," she said. "Some of the poems are about the ocean."

I opened the book. The pictures were beautiful, but some of the words weren't familiar to me.

"Would you like me to read one to you?" asked the librarian.

I nodded.

She sat down beside me and began to read:

Tiny waves cascade against the
sand like tinkling bells.
Great breakers blot the sun and
pound the shore like clashing
cymbals.

Lost in the sounds of the ocean, I jumped when my father tapped me on the shoulder. He signed that it was time to leave.

"I'll check this book out to you and you can take it home," the librarian told me. "Maybe you and your father can read it together. And come back as often as you like. We have lots more words to share!"

I felt happy inside.

When we got back down on the street, the storm had passed and the sky was covered with a blanket of stars.

As we headed toward home, glittering Roman candles shot up from a barge out in the dark ocean.

They exploded overhead in a shower of a million wriggling worms of light.

My father dragged us toward the boardwalk.

The sky lit up with fireworks of dazzling colors and fantastic shapes, turning night into day.

Soon the air was full of buzzing, whistling, popping, and screeching. I covered my ears.

The lights and colors danced across my father's face. He held out his hands, sniffing the air as if to see and taste and touch and smell the sounds of the fireworks he couldn't hear.

After a while, the barge let loose with one last burst: twisting spiders, spinning wheels, glowing waterfalls, and enormous flowers exploded all around us.

Then, just as suddenly as they had begun, the fireworks ended. The stars returned, and the night air was filled with the smell of burning wooden matches. Confetti ashes fell softly like snow.

SODA
FRENCH FRIES
5¢
SALLY'S
ICE CREAM
SODA
10¢
CHICKEN • SHRIMP

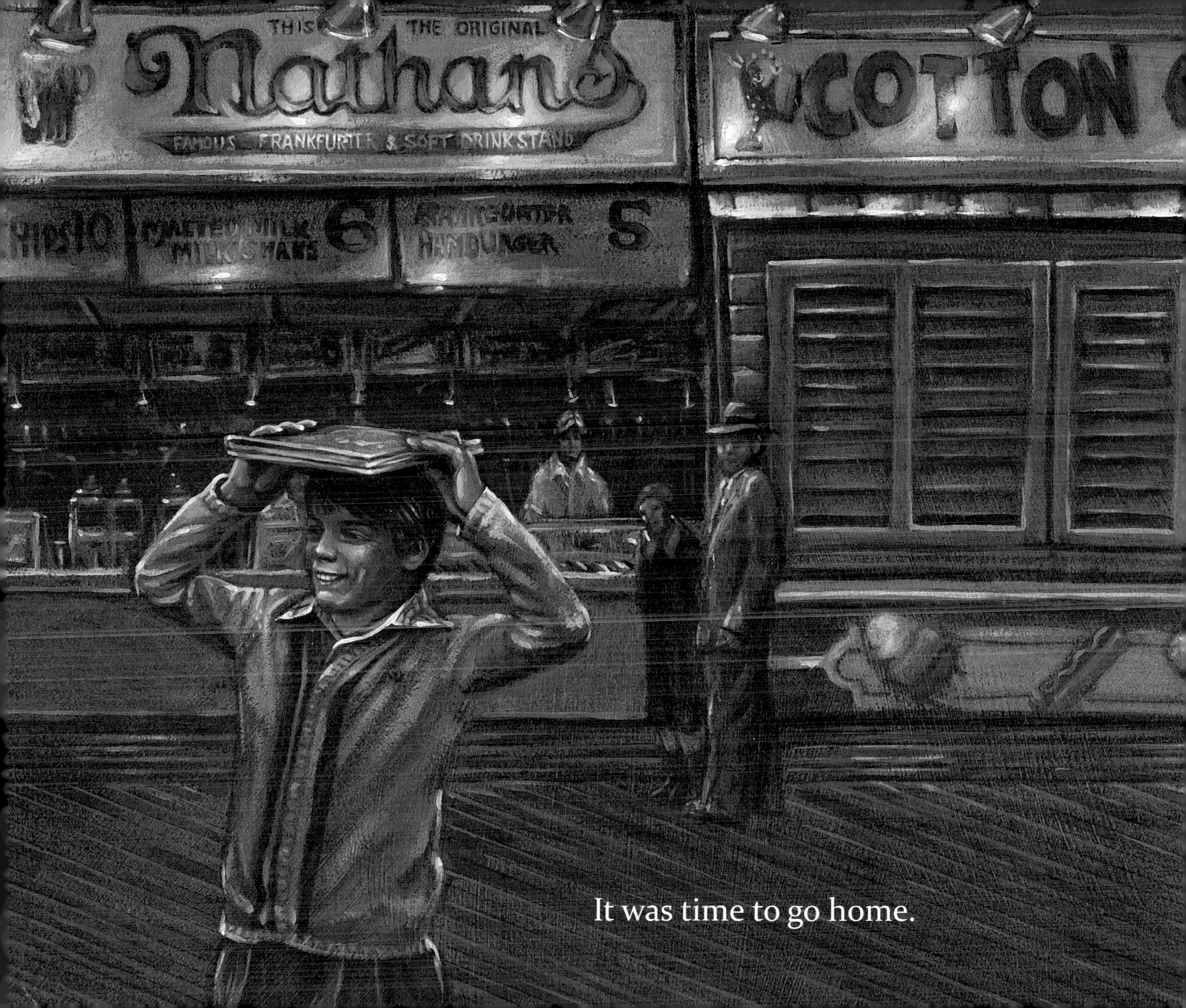

It was time to go home.

After a short subway ride, we climbed the stairs to the street. When we stepped onto the sidewalk, I heard the squeal of an incoming train and felt the rumble under my feet.

I knew my parents could feel that rumbling, too, but not hear the sound.

As we walked home, I tried to imagine what it was like to be deaf. If I closed my eyes, I could imagine being blind. But there was no way I could ever know what it was like being deaf.

Back home in our apartment,
I could hear our neighborhood
through the open window.
Somewhere, a radio was playing.
People were laughing and talking.
A dog barked.

I knew my mother and father
were sitting in their silent world
as they did every evening.

I sat on my windowsill, listening to sounds that my parents would never hear. When the sun rose the next morning, I knew my father would ask me to describe them.

I slowly turned the pages of my new book. I couldn't wait to tell him about the sound of all things.

A Note from the Author

WHEN I WAS A BABY in my crib, I signed my love for my mother and father with my small hands. Signing was my first language because my parents were deaf.

Since I was their first-born child, my parents watched me very carefully, worried that I might lose my hearing as they had. They banged pots and pans near my crib, to reassure themselves that I could hear. Even when I was older, my father would sometimes call my name in his harsh deaf voice: MAH-ROOONNN! And when I turned to the sound of his familiar voice, he would smile.

On our street in Brooklyn, I lived two lives. One was my deaf-life—lived in our silent rooms above the street. Here we spoke with our hands. Below our apartment was my hearing life, lived in the noisy world of the hearing. There I spoke with my mouth. These two worlds, one of silence and the other filled with sound, could never be joined—they were for me forever separate, each wonderful in its own way.

My father dimly remembered a time when he was very young and could hear. But his memories of sound were vague and blurry, like an out-of-focus photograph. And so it was, when I was just a kid, my father asked me to be his interpreter—to explain what the things he saw but couldn't hear sounded like. I didn't understand it then, but now I know that he hoped to experience sound through my ears.

I was proud that my father entrusted me with such an important job. But at first I lacked the words to do it well. I only had the vocabulary of a young child. I did my best. But still my father demanded more. I needed better words and more of them.

Then one day I discovered a place where I could find every word I would ever need—my local library. Here in all these books were the words that I could use to explain the sound of all things for my father.

I am now an old man. My deaf parents died many years ago. But my memories of them will never die; they are as alive as if they happened yesterday. Those memories led me to tell the story of a deaf mother and a deaf father who loved and raised a hearing son in a place called Brooklyn.

I would call their story The Sound of All Things.

—Myron Uhlberg

A Note from the Illustrator

A BIG THANK-YOU to Myron for recommending me to translate his wonderful words and personal story into images. It was my honor to do so. Sincere thanks to Brock Bierly, Curt Middleton, and Kelly Cogan for modeling, and to Bettina and Bob and Mark of Scaramouche Costumes for donating their time. Infinite thanks to all the patient souls at Peachtree Publishers who helped me through this first book project. I could never have completed it without the constant support of my loving wife Drury, her mom's generous help with the newborns Sally and Tess, and my amazing friends and family. A special thank-you to Greg Houston, an extremely talented illustrator, for his consult throughout and enthusiasm for my work and to Dave and Viv for their assistance. I received this project shortly after the passing of my mother, Sally, a talented botanical artist. I inherited her brushes and these were the first works created with them. I love you, Mom. I hope I did your brushes proud.

—Ted Papoulas